For Joshua's lovely teachers—
Lisa Gillitt, Linda Nolan, Joanne Hanley,
Norma Freeman, Margaret O'Neill, Nicola Hadley,
and the children of Yerbury School
*F. S.*

For my friends
Max and Nicola Rabkin
*P. C.*

First published in the United States 1996
by Dial Books for Young Readers
A Division of Penguin Books USA Inc.
375 Hudson Street
New York, New York 10014

Published in Great Britain 1996
by Orion Children's Books
a division of the Orion Publishing Group Ltd
Text copyright © 1996 by Francesca Simon
Pictures copyright © 1996 by Peta Coplans
All rights reserved
Printed in Italy • First Edition
1 3 5 7 9 10 8 6 4 2

Library of Congress Cataloging in Publication Data
Simon, Francesca.
Spider school / Francesca Simon;
pictures by Peta Coplans.—1st ed.
p.  cm.
Summary: Because Kate got out on the wrong side of the bed,
her first day at a new school proves to be a real nightmare,
with a gorilla for a teacher and spiders for lunch.
ISBN 0-8037-1975-2
[1. Nightmares—Fiction. 2. Schools—Fiction.]
I. Coplans, Peta, ill. II. Title.
PZ7.S604Sp 1996 [E]—dc20 95-38293 CIP AC

The art for this book was prepared using
watercolor, crayon, and pen.

# SPIDER SCHOOL

Francesca Simon

*Pictures by* Peta Coplans

Dial Books for Young Readers ▲ New York

Kate sat up in bed. It was the first day of school.

"I don't want to go to a new school," said Kate. "I don't. I don't. **I don't.**"

Kate felt so crabby that she did something she had never done before.

She got out of bed on the wrong side.

Kate looked at the clock. Nine o'clock. She was going to be late. Where oh where was Mom?

Mom ran into the room. "Hurry up and get dressed, Kate!" she shouted. "You'll be late for school!"

Kate ran to the closet. Her new school clothes were gone. Her new school shoes were gone. Her new school socks were gone too.

"Where are my new school clothes, Mom?" asked Kate.
"Gone," said Mom. "You'll have to wear something else."
Kate had to wear a dirty old skirt. Her old socks kept
falling down. Her old shoes were too tight and squeezed
her toes.

"Come on, Kate!" said Mom. They ran down the street. The street was empty. Kate's feet thudded on the pavement.

Clunk-clunk.

Clunk-clunk.

Clunk-clunk.

Then Kate saw her new school. The school was big and dark and ugly. It did not look like a nice school. It looked like a dungeon.

Mom left her at the gate.

"Go to Class 3," she said.

"But where is Class 3?" asked Kate.

"You're a big girl. You'll find it," said Mom.

Kate wandered up the hall. Kate wandered down the hall. She found Class 1, Class 2, Class 4, Class 5, Class 6, and Class 7—but not Class 3.

The other children hurried past her. Everyone knew where they were going—but not Kate.

At last she found Class 3. The door was very big.

Kate knocked.
No one came.
Kate knocked
a little harder.
Still no one came.

Kate knocked on the door as hard as she could.

The door opened.
A gorilla appeared.
## "You're late,"
said the gorilla.
"But where is my teacher?" said Kate.

"Right here, knucklehead," said the gorilla.

All the children stared at Kate as she tiptoed into the classroom. She looked everywhere for her friend Robbie, but he wasn't there.

Kate looked around the room. The children were sitting on the floor.

There were no tables.

There were no chairs.

There were no pencils.

There were no worksheets.

There were no posters.

"Where are the books?" asked Kate.

"No books here," snapped the gorilla.
The children sat still. No one said a word.
The gorilla sat at her desk and read a comic book.

Something is not right, thought Kate.

She raised her hand.

"Yes?" said the gorilla.

"Where are the bathrooms?" asked Kate.

"No bathrooms here," said the gorilla.

The clock ticked loudly. The children sat.

The gorilla read her comic book.

Kate raised her hand.

"Yes?" said the gorilla.

"What are we going to learn today?" asked Kate.

"You want to learn?" said the gorilla. "Okay. What's the first letter of the alphabet?"

"A," said Kate.

"Wrong," said the gorilla. "The first letter of the alphabet is Z. Now be quiet. I'm busy."

Something is very wrong, thought Kate.

The clock struck twelve. Lunchtime. The lunch lady stood behind a big pot.

Inside the pot were snakes and snails and spiders.

"Excuse me," said Kate.

"Yes?" snarled the gorilla.

"I don't like snakes and snails and spiders," said Kate.

"Oh yes, you do," said the gorilla.

"Oh no, I don't," said Kate.

"We don't like snakes and snails and spiders," shouted the children.

"Oh yes, you do," shouted the gorilla.

"Oh no, we don't," shouted the children.

"I won't eat them," said Kate.

"We won't eat them," shouted the children.

"But these spiders are delicious," said the lunch lady. "And so good for you. Try one with tomato sauce." And she popped a spider into her mouth.

"Delicious," said the lunch lady. "Try one, Kate." And she dangled a big black spider in front of her.

Kate screamed. "I don't want a spider! I don't want to be at this horrible spider school! I WANT TO GO HOME!"

Kate ran home as fast as she could. She ran to her
bedroom, took off her clothes, put on her pajamas, jumped
into bed, pulled the covers over her head, and closed her eyes.

Then Kate sat up, took a deep breath, and got out of bed.

But this time she got out on the right side.

The sun was shining. Mom peeped in the door.

"Am I late for school?" asked Kate.

"No," said Mom. "It's only seven o'clock."

Kate felt very happy.

Kate put on her new school clothes, ate breakfast, and walked to school with Mom.

Kate's teacher met them at the door. "Hello, Kate. Welcome to our school," said her teacher. "I'm Mrs. Miller."

Class 3 was cheery and bright. There were tables and chairs. There were pencils and worksheets for Kate. And there was her friend Robbie, reading in the book corner.

"Here's the coatroom, where we hang our coats and hats," said Mrs. Miller. "And here are the bathrooms."

And the school lunch?
Kate had peas, carrots, chicken, and French fries.
No snakes, no snails, no spiders.

Well, hardly any.